P9-CNH-773

OBSOLETE

one HOT summer day

Nina Crews

Greenwillow Books, New York

To my family and friends who have shared my hot summer days

Special thanks to Joy Elaine Henry, who modeled for the book, and her great-grand-parents James and Margie Wilson. Also thanks to Donald and Ann Crews for all of their help and advice.

The art was prepared as collages made from color photographs that were taken and printed by the author. The text type is Franklin Gothic. Copyright © 1995 by Nina Crews. All rights reserved. No part of this book may be reproduced or utilized in any form or by any means, electronic or mechanical, including photocopying, recording, or by any information storage and retrieval system, without permission in writing from the Publisher, Greenwillow Books, a division of William Morrow & Company, Inc., 1350 Avenue of the Americas, New York, NY 10019.
Printed in Hong Kong by South China Printing Company (1988) Ltd.
First Edition 10 9 8 7 6 5 4 3

Library of Congress Cataloging-in-Publication Data
Crews, Nina.
One hot summer day / by Nina Crews.
    p.   cm.
Summary: Relates a child's activities in the heat of a summer day punctuated by a thunderstorm.
ISBN 0-688-13393-2 (trade)
ISBN 0-688-13394-0 (lib. bdg.)
[1. Summer—Fiction.] I. Title.
PZ7.C86830n 1995   [E]—dc20
94-6268   CIP   AC

It's summer, and it's hot.

Dogs pant.
Hydrants are open.
Women carry umbrellas
for the shade.

**Hot enough to fry an egg
on the sidewalk.**

Well, maybe not.

My mother tells me
to play inside games.
She has the fan on high.

Instead, I stand outside
and tease my shadow.

Then I run into the shade and draw pictures.

It's too hot to play
on the swings or
in the sandbox.

I eat two
grape Popsicles
in a row.

I look at the sky.
It's getting dark and cloudy.

Thunder comes,
and then big drops.

I dance in the rain.

I sing in the rain.

I splash in the rain.

The rain stops.

It's nice and cool.
I run to the playground,
and I swing high.